For my lovely Dad, sorry for never walking my puppy, despite sending you a signed letter promising that I would! – C.E.

For the little beavers, Soren and Iris xx – D.T.

With very special thanks to the children of class 3C, Cosby Primary School, Leicestershire, and the children of Catherine Emmett, for their wonderful 'Pet' drawings.

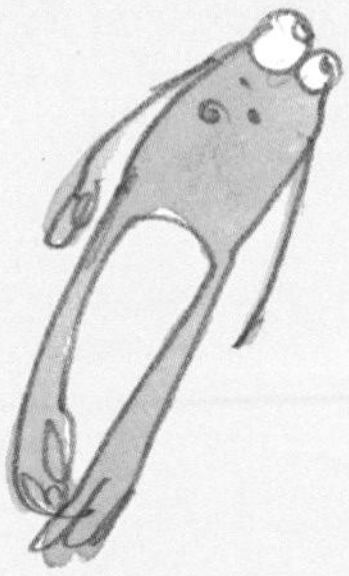

First published 2021 by Macmillan Children's Books
an imprint of Pan Macmillan
The Smithson, 6 Briset Street, London EC1M 5NR
EU representative: Macmillan Publishers Ireland Limited,
Mallard Lodge, Lansdowne Village, Dublin 4
Associated companies throughout the world
www.panmacmillan.com

Hardback ISBN: 978-1-5098-9529-8
Paperback ISBN: 978-1-5098-9531-1

1 3 5 7 9 8 6 4 2

A CIP catalogue record for this book is available from the British Library.
Printed in China

FSC www.fsc.org
MIX
Paper from responsible sources
FSC® C116313

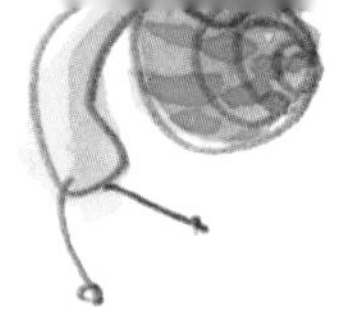

CAUTIONARY TALES
FOR CHILDREN AND GROWN-UPS

The Pet

Catherine Emmett

David Tazzyman

Macmillan Children's Books

Digby David slammed the door,
And dumped his bag upon the floor.

**"Daddy! I demand a pet,
Why have I not got one yet?
Reuben's got a guinea pig,
I want one that's twice as big!"**

Daddy's hair turned slightly grey,
"I'll call the pet shop right away!"

"**I want this one!**" Digby said.

The pet shop owner shook her head.
"This guinea pig has such long hair,
She must be groomed with special care."
Digby's face turned violent red,
"We'll pay double!" Daddy said.

So now that Digby had his way,

He loved his pet . . .

. . . for half a day.

But guinea pigs don't *do* that much –
So Digby left her in her hutch.

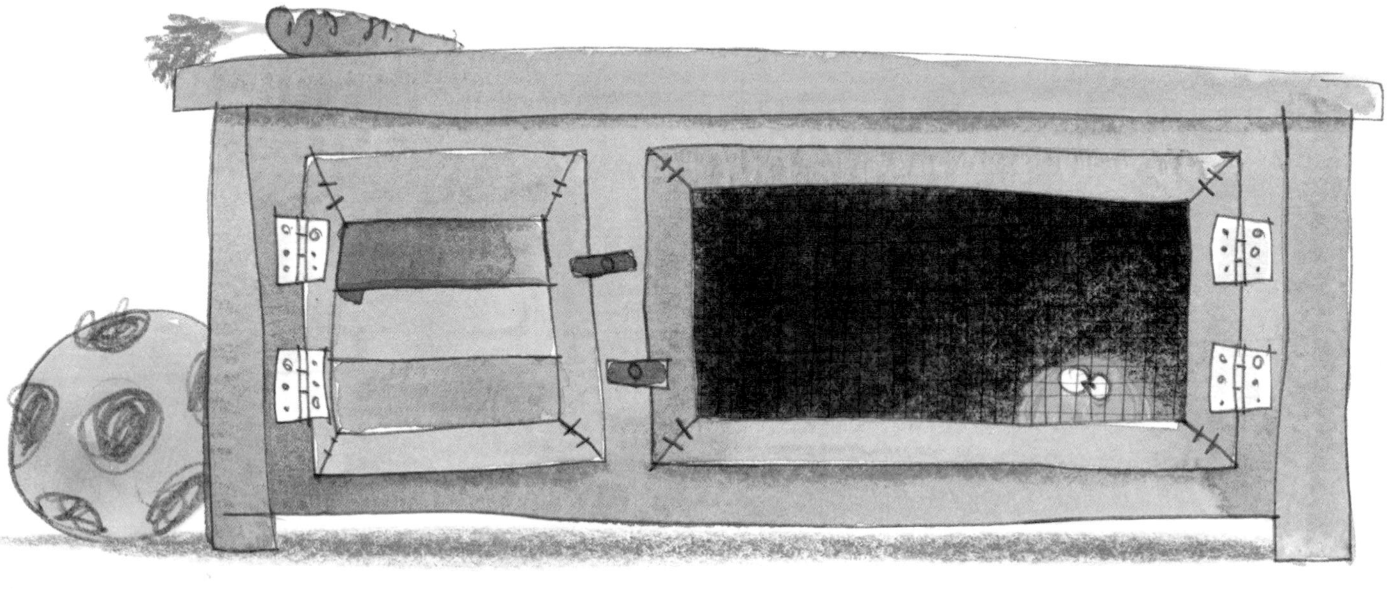

"Lily Jean has got a cat!
My pet's not half as good as that."
Digby stormed, **"She says it purrs,**
I want a better pet than hers!"

Daddy's hair turned slightly grey,
"I'll call the pet shop right away!"

"I want **that one!**" Digby said.
The pet shop owner shook her head.
"That dog needs walks three times a day,
I'm sorry but there's just no way–"

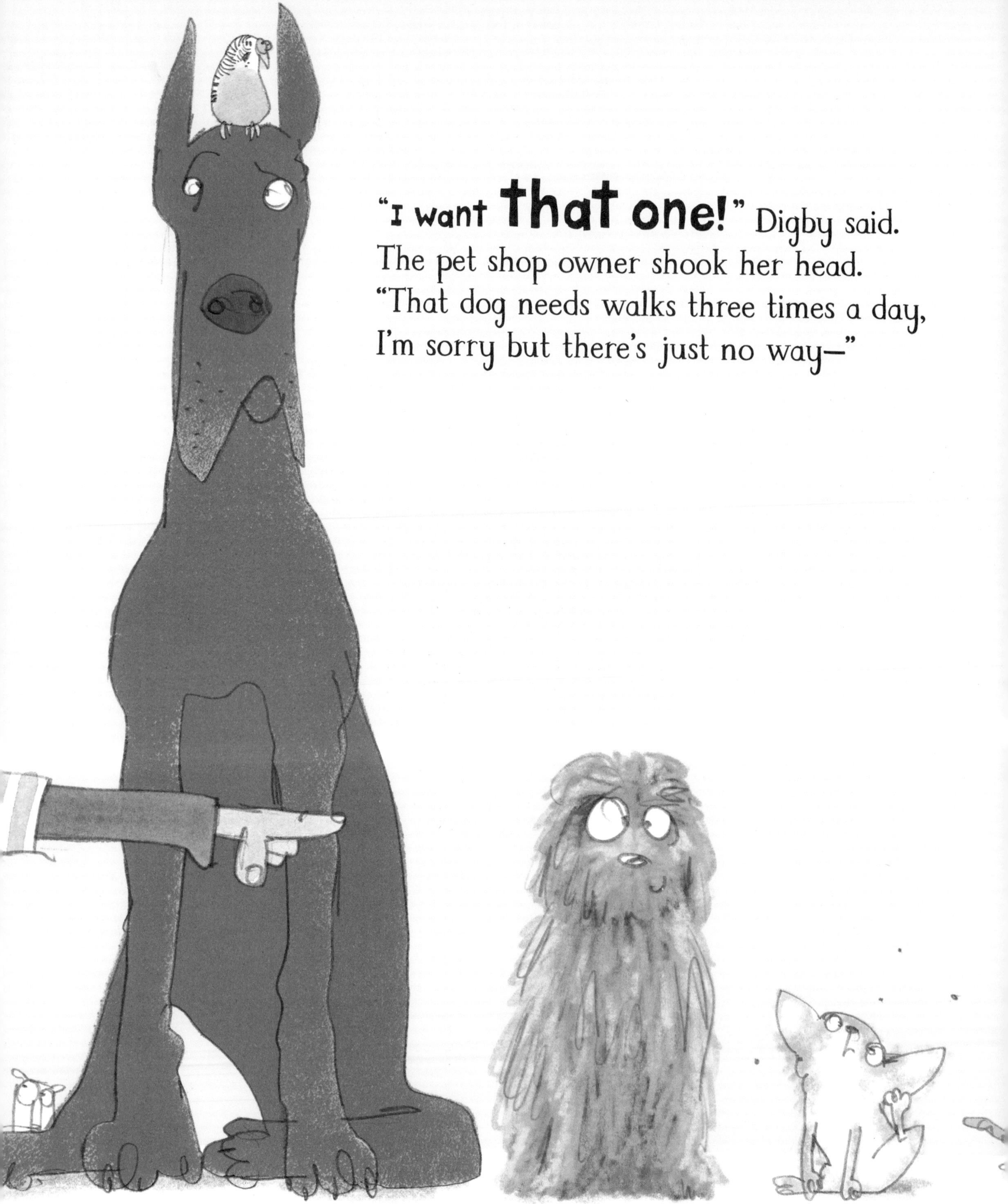

Digby's face turned violent red,
"We'll pay triple!" Daddy said.

So Digby walked his dog that day,
But later Henry came to play . . .

To go outside was such a chore,
So Digby's dog was walked no more.

Digby yelled, "**Don't want my dog!**
Lola says she's got a frog.
Dipak says that he's got three!
They've both got better pets than me!"

Daddy's hair turned slightly grey,
"I'll call the pet shop right away!"

"Don't want a dog, or frog OR rat
Daddy, Daddy! I want THAT!"

The pet shop owner shook her head,
"Oh no!" she very firmly said.
"You'd have to feed him twice a day
And let him out to have a play.

GUS
BANANAS

"For if he's left
alone too long,
Well, things can really
go quite wrong . . ."

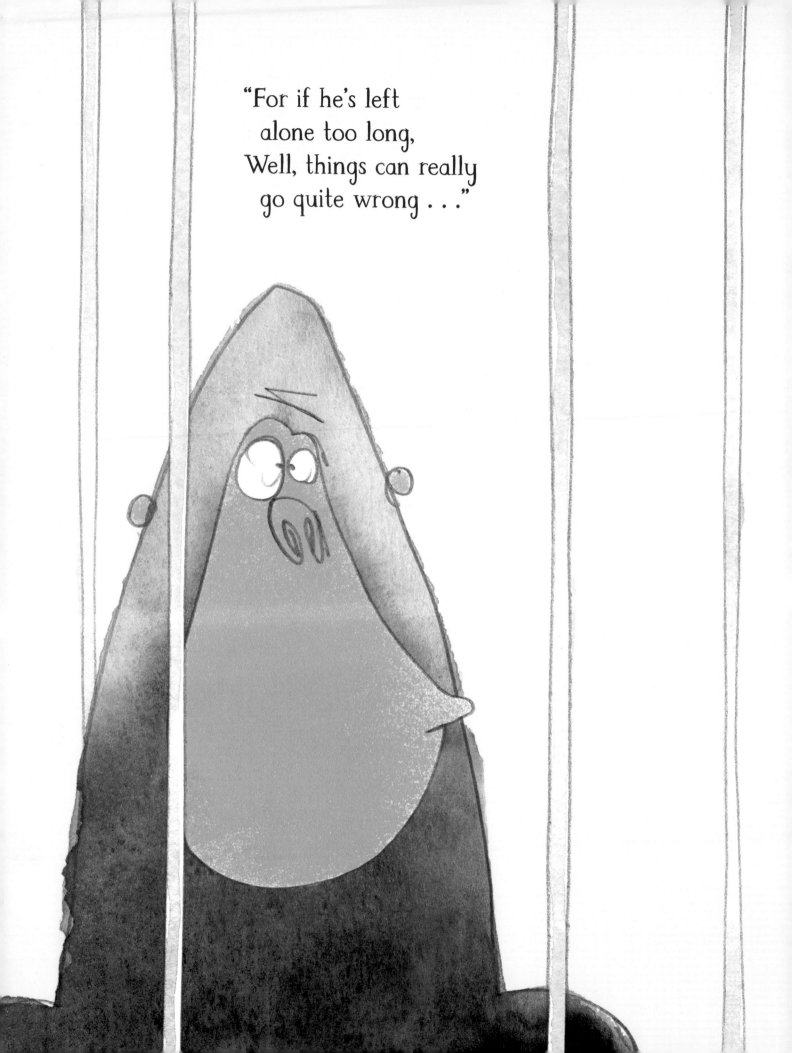

Digby's face turned violent red,
"Take all my money!" Daddy said.

So Digby LOVED his
brand new pet –
by far the best one
he'd had yet.

He boasted to his friends at school
That his pet Gus was super cool.

He fed him every other day,
And sometimes let him out to play.
But soon poor Gus was just ignored,

And soon poor Gus grew very bored . . .

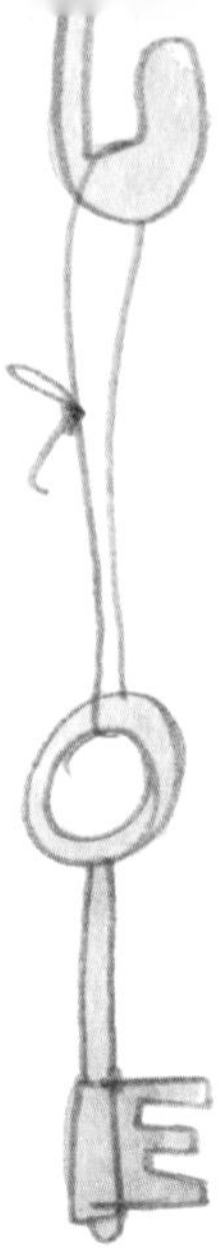

So plotting how he could break free,
Gus noted where they kept the key.

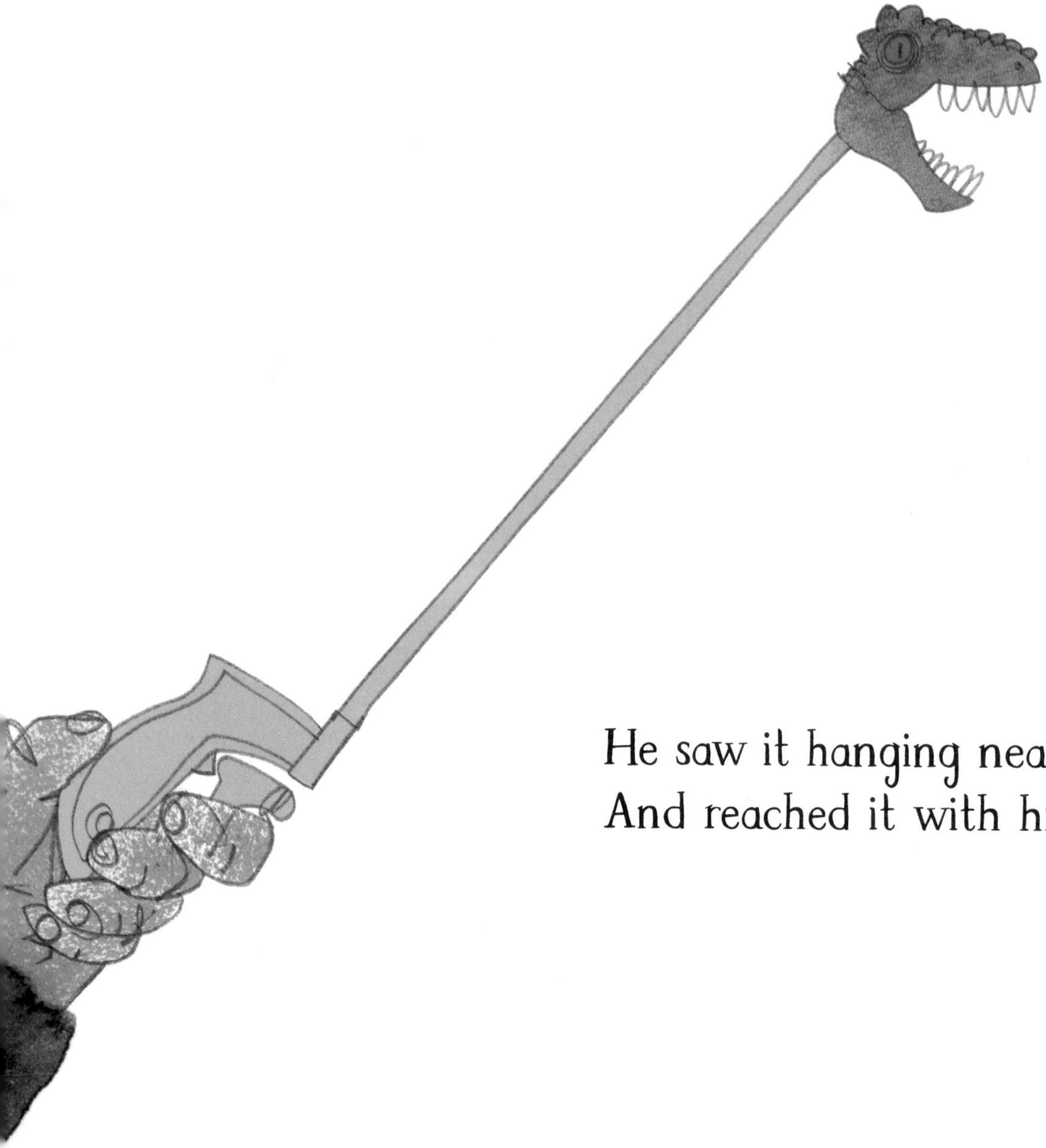

He saw it hanging near his door,
And reached it with his hairy paw.

The unlocked door swung open wide
And Gus was free! He leapt outside . . .

He tidied Digby's toys away,
And walked the dog
three times that day.

And though his hairy hands were big,
He gently groomed the guinea pig.

When Digby saw the empty cage
He flew into a red-faced rage!

At first poor Gus drew back in fear,
But then he had a bright idea . . .

When Daddy made it home that night,
He'd never witnessed such a sight . . .

For Digby's room was nice and neat,
And 'Digby' seemed (for once) quite sweet.

He went to bed when he was told.
In fact he was as good as gold!

The REAL Digby was happy too,
For Gus 'rehomed' him at the zoo.

So please be warned and don't forget –
Make sure you don't neglect your pet!